It's a Wild life, buddy!

Daniela De Luca

Lizzie
THE ELEPHANT

Tommy NELSON®

ON A SHADY AFRICAN SAVANNA, Mom
shared great news with her daughter Chloe,
Grandma, and Aunt Flora. "I'm expecting
a new baby!" Mom told everyone.

4

DO BABY ELEPHANTS REALLY SUCK THEIR TRUNKS?
Yes, just as children sometimes suck their thumbs for comfort, elephant babies, called calves, sometimes suck their trunks.

DO FEMALE ELEPHANTS REALLY LIVE TOGETHER IN A GROUP?
Yes, they live together in a family herd led by an older female, called a matriarch. Female elephants, or cows, help each other to protect and bring up their young.

5

ONE RAINY DAY SOON
AFTER, Mom was
ready to give birth.
Grandma, Aunt Flo,
Aunt Flora, and the
girls all gathered
around to help.

DO ELEPHANTS REALLY WASH THEMSELVES?
Yes, elephants have sensitive skins, which the cool water soothes. They like to roll in mud and suck up water in their trunks and spray it over themselves and their friends!

DO THEY TAKE DUST BATHS TOO?
Yes, the dust also makes their skins feel good and it helps to keep bugs away.

Mom

Grandma

Chloe

EVERY DAY LIZZIE AND HER FAMILY would go to the water hole to drink and bathe. Lizzie loved to run ahead and plunge into the water first. Aunt Flora always brought her beauty case and a scrubbing brush to clean the girls.

10

Aunt Flo, taking a dust bath

Aunt Flora

Zoe

Lizzie

AT LAST, the little elephant was born! It was a little girl. Grandma and Aunt Flora were so excited! Mom cuddled her new daughter. "I'll call you Lizzie," she whispered.

WHEN ARE ELEPHANT CALVES BORN?
In the "rainy" season, when there is lots of new grass for the mother elephant to eat.

7

AFTER HER BATH, Lizzie wandered off while gathering flowers. She sang as she went and followed a dancing butterfly far into the bush.

WHY DO BIRDS FOLLOW ELEPHANTS AS THEY PLOD THROUGH THE BUSH?
Because as they walk through the long grass the elephants disturb insects and other small animals which the birds feed on.

14

Sebastian Leopard

Terry Antelope

Jed and Myra Baboon

Vincent and Rachel Warthog

Flip and Flap Egret

Fred Marabou

12

Fiona
Giraffe

Winston
Giraffe

Fanny and
Dave Rhino

13

A FEW DAYS LATER, Lizzie was out in the bush with Grandma, who was showing her the tastiest plants, as well as poisonous plants that Lizzie should never eat. While Grandma spoke, Lizzie practiced using her trunk to eat.

WHAT DO ELEPHANTS EAT?
They eat grass, leaves, shrubs, twigs, flowers, fruit, and bark. They use their trunks to gather food and carry it to their mouths.

9

BACK AT HOME, the others began to worry about Lizzie. Mom called for her, while Chloe kept watch behind a bush.

WHAT IS AN ELEPHANT "ROAD"?
It is a wide path through the bush made by elephants. They use the same path for generations so it becomes very deep and well-marked. The roads can act as firebreaks and rainwater channels.

DO ELEPHANTS REALLY CALL EACH OTHER?
Yes, elephants can communicate with each other over quite long distances using calls, or rumbles, that are so low-pitched that human ears cannot hear them.

LITTLE LIZZIE sat in the shade of a large rock to rest. She stuck flower petals on her toenails and chattered with the egrets and oxpeckers. Time passed, but Lizzie didn't notice.

WHY DO BIRDS SIT ON ELEPHANTS' BACKS?
Birds like cattle egrets and oxpeckers ride along on elephants because they can peck insects and parasites off their thick skins.

As it grew darker, Lizzie became afraid. She wasn't really sure where she was or how to get back home to her family. *Boom! Bam! Boom! Bam!* Lizzie looked up to see a huge elephant coming toward her. He was so big that the ground shook as he walked. Lizzie was terrified until the elephant roared, "Hello, Lizzie! It's me, Grandpa."

A little bird told me that your mother is looking for you."

17

18

LIZZIE WAS VERY HAPPY to see her grandfather. She skipped along beside him as they made their way home. Suddenly Grandpa stopped and pointed at some bones beside the path. "Look Lizzie," he said. "Those belong to your great grandmother. She was a very wise elephant and a great leader. You should try to be more like her, and not go running off into the bushes on your own."

DO ELEPHANTS REALLY RECOGNIZE BONES?
Yes, they seem to. Elephants will often stop when they see other elephant bones, touching them with their trunks and sometimes tossing them into the air.

JUST AS GRANDPA AND LIZZIE got back to
Lizzie's family, they saw Aunt Flo, Aunt
Flora, and Mom huddling to protect Chloe
and Zoe. Grandma was waving her umbrella
at a lion in a bush and shouting, "Scat!"

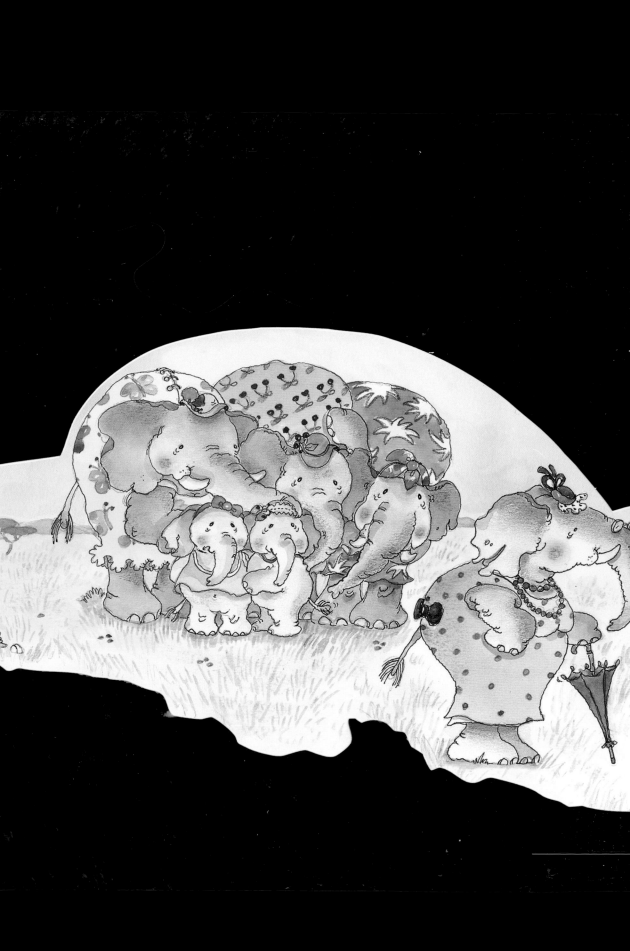

GRANDPA stepped in
quickly and scared
the lion away.

WHAT DO DUNG BEETLES DO?
Some of the seeds that an
elephant eats end up in the
elephant's waste. Dung
beetles carry the waste
underground, and the
seeds then start to grow.

DO ELEPHANTS REALLY GREET EACH OTHER BY RUBBING THEIR TRUNKS TOGETHER?
Yes. When elephants meet, they stand close together and entwine their trunks. They also give each other comforting pats with their trunks throughout the day.

EVERYONE WAS SO HAPPY to see Lizzie back home safely. They wrapped their trunks together in greeting and decided to have a family party. And Lizzie promised never to wander off from her family again.

DID YOU KNOW?

THERE ARE THREE SPECIES of elephants. Two of them live in Africa. They are called African elephants. The third species lives in India and Southeast Asia and is known as the Asian elephant. African elephants are bigger than their Asian cousins and have larger ears. Both males and females have tusks.

ASIAN ELEPHANTS are slightly smaller than the African ones. Usually only the males have tusks. In Asia some elephants are used as work animals or for transport. In India, elephants are often dressed in brightly colored materials and take part in religious parades and festivals.

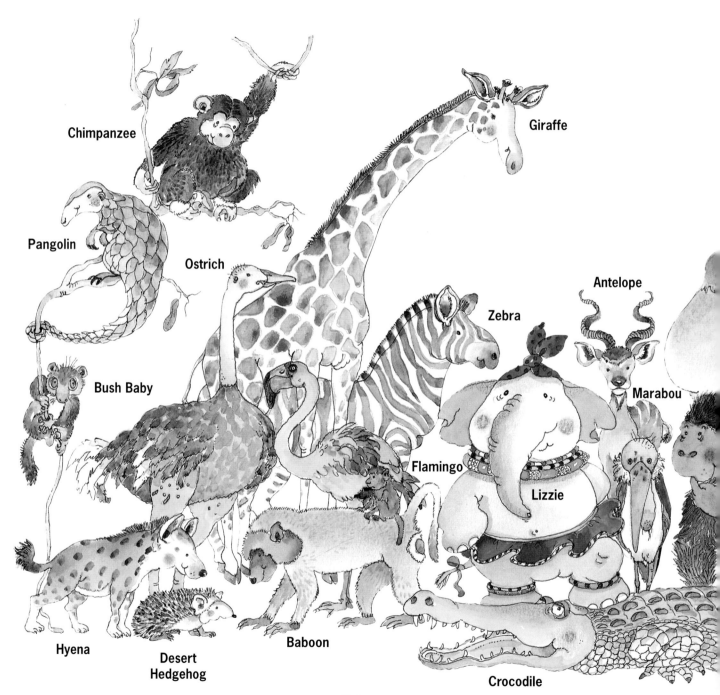

Chimpanzee

Giraffe

Pangolin

Ostrich

Antelope

Zebra

Bush Baby

Marabou

Flamingo

Lizzie

Hyena

Desert
Hedgehog

Baboon

Crocodile

26

LIZZIE AND HER FRIENDS live in Africa. Do you see Lizzie? Do you recognize all her friends?

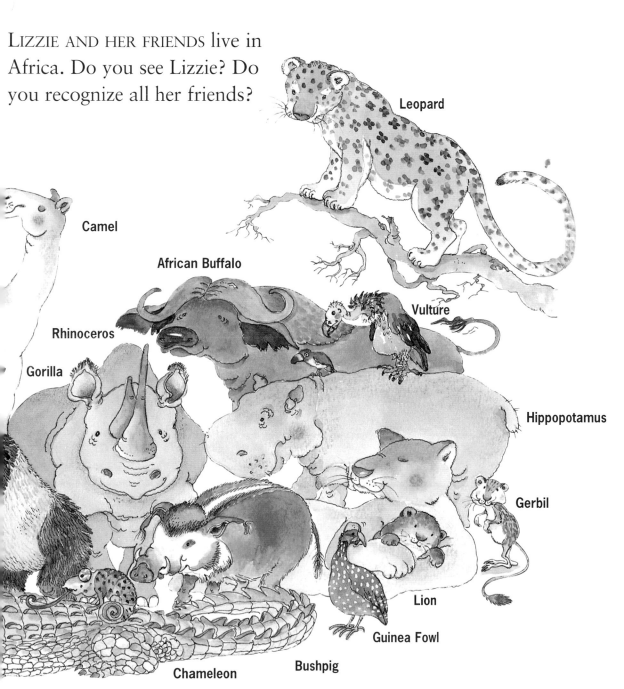

Camel

Leopard

African Buffalo

Vulture

Rhinoceros

Gorilla

Hippopotamus

Gerbil

Lion

Guinea Fowl

Chameleon

Bushpig

So God made the wild animals, the tame animals and all the small crawling animals. . . . God saw that this was good.
Genesis 1:25

Copyright © 2005 McRae Books Srl, Borgo S. Croce, 8 - Florence, Italy
info@mcraebooks.com

ISBN 1-4003-0565-9

Scripture quoted from the *International Children's Bible*®, *New Century Version*®, copyright © 1986, 1988, 1999 by Tommy Nelson®, a Division of Thomas Nelson, Inc., Nashville, Tennessee 37214.

This book was conceived, edited and designed by McRae Books Srl, Florence, Italy.

North American version published by Tommy Nelson®, a Division of Thomas Nelson, Inc.

Publishers: Anne McRae, Marco Nardi
Text: Vicky Egan
Illustrations: Daniela De Luca
Designer: Rebecca Milner, Sebastiano Ranchetti

05 06 07 08 09 - 5 4 3 2 1

Repro: Litocolor, Florence, Italy
Printed and bound in China